This book is dedicated to everyone who has supported my writing journey. I hope the child that reads this book will love (HBCUs) Historical Black College Universities, as much as I do!

Ordering Information:
For details, contact- categbole@gmail.com
Hardback ISBN: 978-1-7366002-2-1

MY HBCU TOUR

CHARLES ATEGBOLE
ILLUSTRATED BY TRAVIS A. THOMPSON

Meet Chase. Chase lives with his mom, dad, sister Natalie and dog Skip.

Chase is excited, because today is a big day! He is going to experience his first college tour. What makes it even better... It's an HBCU! A Historically Black College/University.

Chase's parents are proud HBCU alums, and all they talk about are the memories they have from their college days. Chase is excited, because he will finally get to see what all the fuss is about.

Before the college tour, Chase's dad makes the biggest breakfast and Chase instantly knows what that means. "Dad only cooks like this when he is very excited," he happily thinks to himself. "So, I know today is going to be great day for me!"

During the drive to the college, Chase's mom and dad talk about all the fun, historical facts and life lessons they learned while attending an HBCU.

Once they arrive, Chase gets out the car and grabs his note pad and pencil to take notes. He wants to soak up every piece of knowledge he can during his tour.

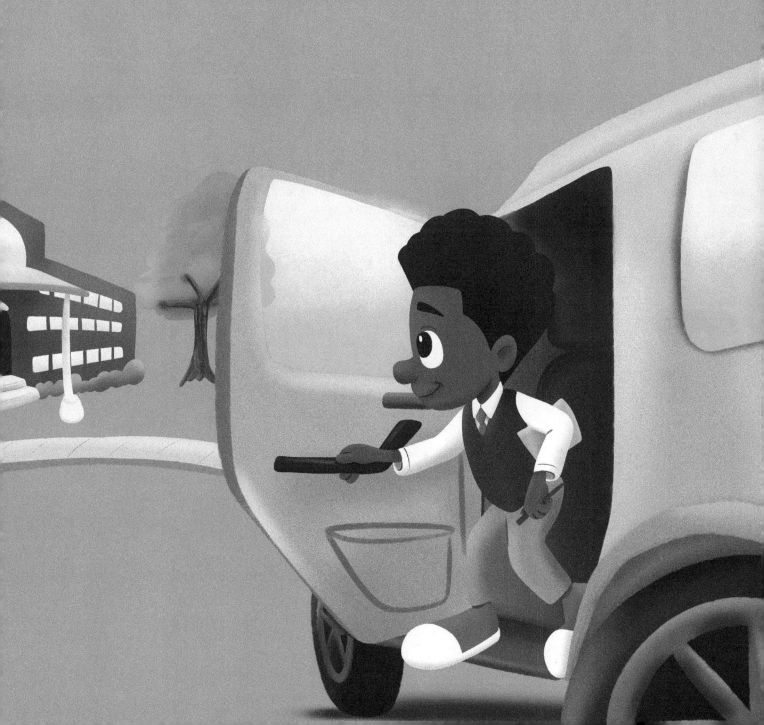

When they get on campus, they are greeted by a huge WELCOME sign on the front lawn. Chase and his parents immediately take a photo to mark the event.

Walking around the campus, Chase is amazed to see so many people that look like him in one place! The students are dressed so nice!

Chase's mom and dad immediately get to work teaching him the names of the important individuals on the buildings-past and present- and the tremendous work they have done for the community as African Americans. Chase is filled with immense pride that every name on each building is named after a person that looks like him.

He is pleasantly taken aback when he walks in a math class and sees everyone actively learning and paying attention! They appear to be as in love with math as he is.

When they get back outside, most of the students are done with their classes and are relaxing, talking and laughing with one another. It feels like home. Like family.

The band is also outside practicing. Looking around, Chase sees so much Black Excellence. He sees students selling an array of items, which instantly makes him think he should've brought some of his chips to sell.

To Chase and his parents' surprise, they run into Chase's dad's frat brother. His father is beyond thrilled to see him and gives him the biggest hug. His dad's friend is making chicken on the grill, and it smells so good, Chase doesn't hesitate to grab a plate!

While the band is playing, the students are
dancing and having a great time. It
reminds Chase of his family's reunions but
with more people and more fun!

Chase is having the time of his life. He can't wait to attend an HBCU!

I'm a proud Alum of Morehouse College class of 2015. Attending a HBCU shaped me into the man I am today, I can say it was the best decision I have ever made! I still talk to most of my Morehouse brothers to this day and also do business with a few. I'm glad Spelman and Clark was right across the street from me where I built great friendships. All colleges in the (AUC) Atlanta played a big role in my life and I'm forever grateful.

CPSIA information can be obtained
at www.ICGtesting.com
Printed in the USA
LVHW061942211022
731268LV00005B/133